QUiRKy QUIZZES

and Weird Word Games

By Howie Dewin

TWISTED PUZZLES, FEROCIOUS FILL-INS, AND MORE!

Scholastic Inc.

ISBN 978-1-338-53759-8

10 9 8 7 6 5 4 3 2 1   19 20 21 22 23

Printed in the U.S.A.   40

First printing 2019

Book design by Kay Petronio

WELCME

TO THE FEISTY WORLD OF FUN AND GAMES!

Whether puzzles make you feel friendly or feisty, you are going to LOVE this book because it's about us—the Feisty Pets! It's packed with puzzles, quizzes, and fill-ins—what could be more fun? All you need is a pen or pencil and your huge brain.

And don't worry: All the answers are in the back . . . though puzzles are usually more fun if you try them out on your own first! But you do you. (We won't judge.)

What are you waiting for?! Turn the page and get puzzlin'! Don't make us get feisty on you!

A SECRET MESSAGE

Here's a message from GLENDA GLITTERPOOP written in a secret code. She's given you a head start by showing you the symbols for all the letters in the words "WE ARE THE FEISTY PETS." Using those letters as a starting point, can you crack the rest of the code and reveal her message?

HINTS:

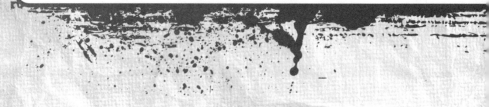

WE   ARE   THE   FEISTY   PETS

__ ___ ____ __ ____ _____

__ ____ _____, ___ _____

___ __ __ ____ __ __ ____ __

◖□● ▲⊠ D⊠ ▲H□▲ ○● ▲⊠ ▲UR▲ ▲O

___ ____ __ ____ ____ ___ ____

▲H■ B□C▲ O● ▲H○● BOO▲ □N✦ LOO▲

__ __ _____. ___ __ __ ___

□▲ ▲H■ □N●◖R●. BU▲ ◖■ D⊠ NO▲

_____ _____ __ _____ ____,

■NDOR●■ CH■□▲ON⊗ O◐ B■ON⊗ L□Z●,

_____ ___ ____ __ __

UNL■●● ●O▽ ◖□N▲ ▲⊠ B■

_ _____ __ _____ ____

□ BLOCKH■□✦ O◐ □ COUC● ■O▲□▲⊠

___ ___ ____ __ ____ ____!

■O◐ ▲H■ R■●▲ O● ●OU◐ LO●■!

MATCH THE FEISTY PET

WITH WHAT THAT FEISTY PET LOVES TO DO!

Billy Blubberbutt

Buford Buttsniffer

Dolly Llama

Ebeneezer Claws

Eating poo

Spitting

Spearfishing

Stealing candy from babies

Kickboxing

Ferdinand Flamefart

Hanging out

Glenda Glitterpoop

Grandmaster Funk

Staring at mirrors

Screaming

Jacked-Up Jackie

Throwing poo

Junkyard Jeff

Playing with fire

Lightning Bolt Lenny

UNSCRAMBLE
THESE FEISTY PET NAMES!

(TIP: All names are at least two words long.)

AAEEHLLLNT

CCIIIKOSUVVY

ACEIILLNTUX

AABBDLNORTTUY

CCDEIILOYZZ (3 words)

ACEIINN'RRS

ADEFFJJKNRUY

CEHIMNOOPPRSSTTTUY

ABBCEKOTWY

AAEEIJRRSSUWZ

CDDEEEIINTTX

ADEFLRU

9

FINISH THE FEISTY HAIKU

Black belt and panda.

Extraordinary bear!

_____

Here's how you do a **HAIKU** . . . The first line is **5** syllables, the second line is **7** syllables, and the third line is **5** syllables. Check out mine below, then write the last line for everyone else's!

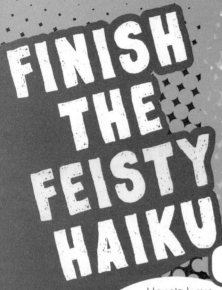

I miss the old days

when my friends were huge like m

_____

EXAMPLE

With wings and a horn,

I'm Ali the alicorn.

It's cool to be me.

I adore my nose.

Life's a festival of smell.

_ _ _ _ _ _ _ _ _ _ _ _

I'm a mad rodent

who hates running in circles.

_ _ _ _ _ _ _ _ _ _ _ _

I love cats and bones.

Cats and bones don't love me back.

_ _ _ _ _ _ _ _ _ _ _ _

High-fashion models

are super-jealous of me.

_ _ _ _ _ _ _ _ _ _ _ _

Throwing poo. Throw poo.

Throw the poo-poo-poo-poo-poo.

_ _ _ _ _ _ _ _ _ _ _ _

WILD WORD SEARCH

```
W Y O V V Y F E D L Q Z T D B
Y P R L I M T E C U I B R Y R
Y K E E H C T S A P R V K Y A
M A C G T I I R I A D S E S S
O P U U R S R O Z E I S F L S
U O M I L E V E U R F S I Y Y
T Z P W L P N L F S Y E E K P
H S Y S T U G E B M Y L R N P
Y E O B R A S H R F R R Y U E
V M S U O I C O R E F A E P P
E S A S S Y T E W C G E C S K
K Q F C Z S S B O L D F R J D
Y C U A S H E L A F D E E A C
D A Y S C R A P P Y Z F I X L
G R I T T Y R E N R O D F Z T
```

BLUSTERY
BOLD
BRASH
BRASSY
BRAZEN
CHEEKY
FEARLESS
FEISTY
FERAL
FEROCIOUS
FIERCE
FIERY
FRESH
FRISKY
GRITTY
GUTSY
LIVELY
MOUTHY
ORNERY
PEPPY
PLUCKY
QUARRELSOME
SASSY
SAUCY
SCRAPPY
SPIRITED
SPUNKY
STORMY
TOUGH
VICIOUS

"Feisty" is not the only word that describes us!

13

THESE STORIES ARE A PROBLEM!

1. Nellie was born on December 28, 2012. However, her birthday always happens in the middle of summer. How is that possible?

2. Two mothers and two daughters want to take a bike ride. They go to the store and each buys a new bike. The store sells a total of three bikes. How is that possible?

3. What is the best thing to keep in the summer?

4. If Sid was five times as old as Linda five years ago and now he's only three times older than she is, how old is he now?

5. Bobby is two years old. Mary is thirteen years old. Jamie is ten years old. Harry is eight years old. Nikki is fourteen years old. How old is Polly?

6. A tomato costs 45 cents. A carrot costs 50 cents. An onion costs 35 cents. A potato costs 45 cents. A cucumber costs 65 cents. How much does a zucchini cost?

FEROCIOUS FILL-INS

Create a list of words using the prompts below. Then turn the page and use those words to fill in the blanks, creating a feisty story!

ADJECTIVE _____

WEATHER TYPE _____

PLACE _____

ACTIVITY _____

ACTIVITY _____

ACTIVITY _____

TIME _____

MEAL _____

FOOD _____

NUMBER _____

FOOD _____

NUMBER _____

EMOTION _____

FEISTY PET _____

FEISTY PET _____

TYPE OF SPORT _____

EXCLAMATION _____

SIZE ADJECTIVE _____

BODY PART _____

ADVERB _____

VERB WITH "ING" ENDING _____

_____

SIZE ADJECTIVE _____

NOUN _____

COOKING TYPE* _____

PLURAL NOUN _____

SPORTING EVENT _____

* For example: grilled, sautéed, baked . . .

15

A FEISTY PICNIC!

Sammy Suckerpunch and Princess Pottymouth had _____ [ADJECTIVE]

plans for their weekend. Since the forecast was for _____, [WEATHER TYPE]

it was a no-brainer they would head to the _____. Because [PLACE]

then they could _____, _____, and _____. [ACTIVITY] [ACTIVITY] [ACTIVITY]

Plus, they each got to choose one thing they would bring for

_____ _____. Since all cats like _____, [TIME] [MEAL] [FOOD]

Princess brought _____. And since all dogs like [NUMBER]

_____, Sammy brought _____. [FOOD] [NUMBER]

When they got there, they were _____ to see that [EMOTION]

_____ and _____ were already there. Turns out [FEISTY PET] [FEISTY PET]

they landed right in the middle of a _____ competition. [TYPE OF SPORT]

"_____!" shouted Sammy. "With my _____ [EXCLAMATION] [SIZE ADJECTIVE]

_____, I'll win this thing for sure!" He demonstrated by [BODY PART]

_____ _____ through the air and landing on a [ADVERB] [VERB WITH "ING" ENDING]

_____ _____. [SIZE ADJECTIVE] [NOUN]

"What's the prize?" Princess asked.

"_____ _____!" their friends exclaimed. [COOKING TYPE] [PLURAL NOUN]

"Perfect," giggled Princess as she settled in to watch the

_____. [SPORTING EVENT]

OBSERVATION CHALLENGE

Put your powers of observation to the feisty test. Stare at this Feisty Pet scene. When you think you've really studied all the details in this picture, turn the page.

HERE'S THE SAME PICTURE . . . ALMOST!

There are five differences between the picture on the previous page and this one. Can you find them?

Go Figure!

Figure out the patterns used in these lines of numbers. Then, fill in the missing number in the sequence.

A. 0   4   8   ___   16   20

B. 31   30   28   24   ___   0

Figure out which of these numbers is OUT of sequence, and circle it.

C. 8   16   24   32   38   48

D. 321   432   534   654   765   876

What number goes in the empty spot?

E. 6 42 7

3 27 9

8 48 6

5 _5 7

KOOKY CROSSWORD

Each clue is the name of a Feisty Pet, and each answer is the type of creature that Feisty Pet is. Can you fill them all in?

ACROSS

2. Princess Pottymouth
3. Sir Growls-a-Lot
8. Ice Cold Izzy
10. Junkyard Jeff
11. Glenda Glitterpoop
12. Tony Tubbalard
14. Liza Loca
15. Buford Buttsniffer
17. Ginormous Gracie
19. Lunatic Lexi
20. Katy Cobweb
22. Taylor Truelove
28. Dastardly Daniel
29. Henry Whodunnit
30. Suzie Swearjar
31. Lethal Lena
35. Scarin' Erin
37. Ferdinand Flamefart
38. Louie Ladykiller
40. Rascal Rampage

DOWN

1. Vicky Vicious
2. Brainless Brian
4. Mary Monstertruck
5. Billy Blubberbutt
6. Jacked-Up Jackie
7. Black Belt Bobby
9. Cuddles von Rumblestrut
13. Extinct Eddie
16. Sammy Suckerpunch
18. Freddy Wreckingball
21. Lady Monstertruck
23. Sparkles Rainbowbarf
24. Ali Cornball
25. Grandmaster Funk
26. Evil Eden
27. Lightning Bolt Lenny
32. Dolly Llama
33. Karl the Snarl
34. Rude Alf
36. Marky Mischief
39. Sly Sissypants

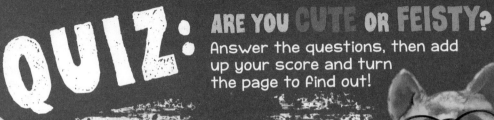

QUIZ: ARE YOU CUTE OR FEISTY?

Answer the questions, then add up your score and turn the page to find out!

What's your FIRST thought in the morning?

1.
1. What a beautiful day to be alive!
2. Five more minutes, please.
3. Ugh. Is it Saturday yet?
4. Wake me up when the mayhem starts!

When someone says, "HAVE A NICE DAY!" what do you say back?

2.
1. Thank you! I hope you have a nice day too!
2. Thanks. You too.
3. Whatever.
4. You talkin' to me?!

If you accidentally got TWO desserts in your lunch, what would you do?

3.
1. Tell the lunch lady and say "thank you" when I return it.
2. Don't tell anyone and keep it between my closest friends.
3. Eat them.
4. Try and get a third one.

What's your opinion of GYM?

4.
1. I always have clean gym clothes and play to the very best of my ability.
2. Some days good, some days not.
3. I'll get a note from my doctor so I don't have to play.
4. I treat every class like it's gym class!

What's your idea of a perfect FIELD TRIP?

5.
1. Lots of worksheets to go with the scientific information given by the tour guide.
2. Amusement park.
3. Lots of bus snacks and no walking.
4. Just give me the keys and I'll *show* you a great field trip!

What's the FIRST THING you do after school?

6.
1. Go to my violin/dance/piano lesson.
2. Stare at the TV and eat cookies.
3. Figure out who will do my homework for me.
4. After? Who went to school?

When you get to choose your piece of CAKE from a buffet, which do you choose?

7.
1. I wait until everyone has taken theirs and happily take what's left.
2. The one closest to me with the most frosting.
3. The biggest one, duh.
4. Choose? I take it all.

When do you do your HOMEWORK?

8.
1. At the first free moment I have, and I don't stop until it's done.
2. Not as soon as I should, but not so late that I can't.
3. I figure out the last possible moment I can wait, then count back five minutes.
4. When? Don't you mean, "Do?" as in, "DO you do your homework?"

How important are GOOD MANNERS at the dinner table?

9.
1. Good manners are the sign of a civilized society.
2. Depends who else is at the table.
3. Try not to spill on anyone you're not related to.
4. *BUUURP!*

What is your first thought when you're told it's time to go to BED?

10.
1. I know. Thanks for reminding me! I'm just brushing my teeth now.
2. Uh-oh. Homework is not done.
3. Make sure my headphones and flashlight are under my pillow.
4. I'm sorry, who are you? And what are you asking me?

SCORING:

For every time you chose answer 1, add 1 to your score.
For every time you chose answer 2, add 2 to your score.
For every time you chose answer 3, add 3 to your score.
For every time you chose answer 4, add 4 to your score.

RESULTS

WHERE DO YOU FALL ON THE FEIST-O-METER?

 35 TO 40: ——— FULL-ON FEISTY

25 TO 34: ——— FEISTY UNTIL I KNOW YOU BETTER

 15 TO 24: ——— CUTE UNLESS PROVOKED

UP TO 14: ——— CUTE 24/7

FULL-ON FEISTY

You are feisty through and through! Inside and outside, up and down, you are so authentically feisty that some might say you're out of control. But people love you for it! Some might call it spunk or gumption, but make no mistake—it's PURE FEISTY!

FEISTY UNTIL I KNOW YOU BETTER

Most anyone who's met you would say you are feisty! Because more often than not, you walk around wearing a feisty disguise and give off lots of feisty attitude. But most anyone who's really gotten to know you would say your feisty is just on the surface. Underneath, you are a kindhearted mush.

CUTE UNLESS PROVOKED

Nine times out of ten you will turn the other cheek when someone behaves badly or a situation doesn't go your way. "Sweet" and "kind" are words most people would use to describe you. BUT, watch out for the TENTH time out of ten, because every now and then, a tough situation brings out your FEISTY!

CUTE 24/7

When it comes to patience and kindness and understanding, you are the person your friends turn to. No matter how frustrating a person or a situation is, you always take a positive point of view and make lemonade from lemons.

OPTICAL ILLUSIONS

Feisty Pets are already their own kind of optical illusion. What are you looking at—is he happy or mad? Is she cute or scary? Now add these pictures to the confusion!

Ferdinand Flamefart is burning everything in sight. How many candles did he light up here?

Rascal Rampage likes eating out of the trash, but that doesn't mean he doesn't have manners. How many tines are on his fork?

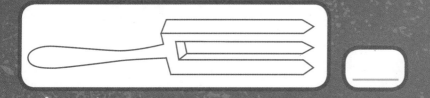

Black Belt Bobby is chopping boards in half everywhere he goes. How many boards is he looking at here?

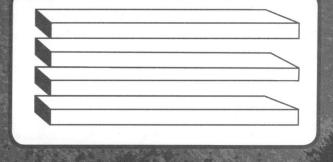

MAGIC? ONLY WE KNOW FOR SURE . . .

Step up, follow the instructions below, and be amazed! Be very amazed!

 Pick a number from 1 to 9.

 Subtract 5. (If you end up with a number less than zero, ignore the negative.)

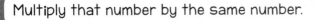 Multiply by 3.

Multiply that number by the same number.

Add the digits until you get a single digit. (For example, 64 → 6 + 4 = 10... then, 10 → 1 + 0 = 1.)

6. If you end up with a number that is less than 5, add 5 to it. Otherwise, subtract 4 from it.

7. Multiply by 2.

8. Subtract 6.

9. Map the digit to a letter in the alphabet (1=A, 2=B, 3=C, etc.).

10. Pick a country that begins with that letter.

11. Take the second letter in the country name and think of a mammal that begins with that letter.

12. Think of the color of that mammal.

DID YOU GET

the same answer as the one that's printed on page 58? Are you amazed by us? We are! Totally amazed by us.

RIDICULOUS REBUSES

Ever done a **REBUS** puzzle before? Just figure out what these phrases are from the way the words are positioned on the page. Then you can say, "YES! I've done a rebus puzzle before!"

1.

```
        G
  G           O
N                 O
    I       F
```

2.

```
R
E
T
T
A
B
```

3.

```
T
H
E
S        U
P        N
R
I
N
K
L
E
R
```

4\.

W

G O

N R

I K

5\.

LYING

THE BEACH

6\.

OATH

LYING

7\.

BEING

TIME

8\.

WATER

SWIMMING

9\.

S S

I I

D D

E E

MAZE MADNESS

Princess Pottymouth is out for a joyride in her convertible. Help her get where she's going!

TO LUNCH WITH HER FEISTY FRIENDS:

start

finish

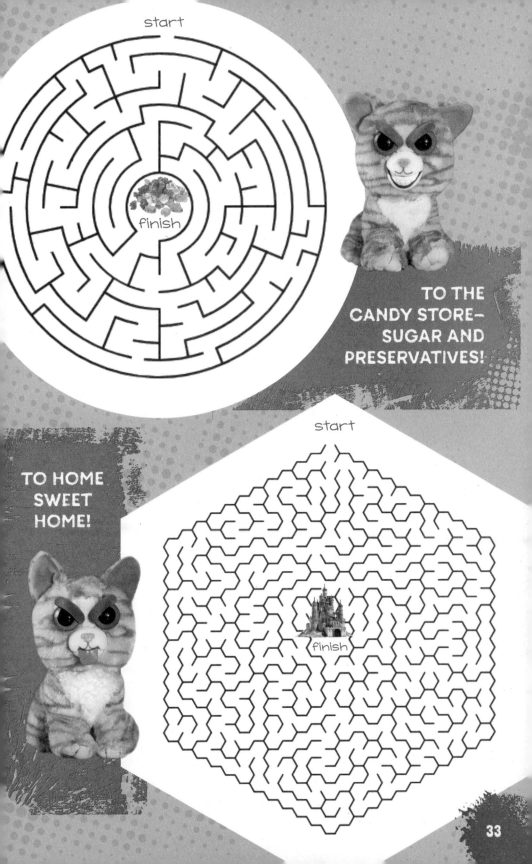

start

finish

TO THE
CANDY STORE—
SUGAR AND
PRESERVATIVES!

TO HOME
SWEET
HOME!

start

finish

33

WACKY WORD GAMES

The sentences in the speech bubbles each have two different missing words that use the same letters as each other. Can you complete the sentences?

I wanted candy to _ _ _ but all they gave m was _ _ _ !

I _ _ _ _ you to call me "_ _ _ _ !"

I like to make noise by banging on _ _ _ _ until my mom screams, "_ _ _ _ !"

I don't copy because I don't want the _ _ _ _ _ _ _ _ to think I'm a _ _ _ _ _ _ _ _ _ !

34

1. Which of these Feisty Pets doesn't belong in this group?

 DANIEL   GRACIE   LIZA

 HENRY   IZZY   BRIAN

 ALI   ERIN   BILLY

2. These three Feisty Pets have something in common:

 DOLLY LLAMA

 FREDDY WRECKINGBALL

 HENRY WHODUNNIT

Which one of these Feisty Pets could join the group?

 LIZA LOCA

 TONY TUBBALARD

 LIGHTNING BOLT LENNY

WILD ABOUT WORDS

These are all words people might use when describing someone who's FEISTY!

F_ _n_
(You make me laugh!)

_ _ E_ _ _ _ _ _ _ _
(There is no forgiving your behavior!)

I_r_ _ _ t_ _ _
(You rub me the wrong way!)

S_ _ _ _
(Wash your mouth out!)

_ _ _ _ _ T_
(This is no way to get on Santa's nice side!)

_ _ _ _ y
(You and pepper would go together perfectly!)

_ _ _ r_ _ P_ _ _ _ _
(You are not treating me honorably!)

_ _ _ E_ _ _ _
(Your behavior is rude!)

T_ _ _ _ _ _ _ _
(When you're extraordinarily great!)

S_ _ _ _
(You're just plain goofy!)

Princess Pottymouth thought you might like a few more hints, so she's written in a few letters!

FEISTY PETS RULE

1. _____
2. _____
3. _____
4. _____
5. _____
6. _____
7. _____
8. _____
9. _____
10. _____
11. _____
12. _____
13. _____
14. _____
15. _____
16. _____
17. _____
18. _____
19. _____
20. _____
21. _____
22. _____
23. _____
24. _____
25. _____
26. _____
27. _____
28. _____
29. _____
30. _____

SCORING:

10-14	You've got attitude.
15-19	You're salty.
20-25	You're feisty!
26 or more	YOU'RE LIVIN' THE FEISTY LIFE!!!

VEXING VISUALS

These feisty friends insist that you can turn their pyramid upside down by only asking three of them to move. Which three would you ask and where would they have to go to make this pyramid stand on its head?

Which Feisty Pets do you think would have which license plate?
Draw a line between each Feisty Pet and its license plate.

I GROWL

I AM QT

TRTLPWR

SLOGO

18POOP

TOP R8D

WHOOOOOO

I B IC

 Ice Cold Izzy

 Henry Whodunnit

 Ali Cornball

 Buford Buttsniffer

 Lightning Bolt Lenny

 Louie Ladykiller

 Glenda Glitterpoop

Sir Growls-a-Lot

Take the quiz below, choosing the response to each question that sounds most like what you'd say. Then add up your score and turn the page to find out which of these four mystery Feisty Pets you're most like!

1. Is it hard to know how you will **REACT** to things?

1. I'm . . . not . . . really . . . very . . . complicated. . .
2. What's to know? It's all about me, right?
3. NOBODY EVER WONDERS WHAT I THINK!
4. Yup. Nope. Maybe. Yup. Maybe. OK. Yo! Yo!

2. Is it better to **LOOK** good than to **FEEL** good?

1. Mirrors are exhausting.
2. What's the question?
3. I say, just get the job done now!
   Look in the mirror later!
4. I can do both.

3. Would others call you a **LEADER**?

1. I don't believe in leading or following.
2. Hahahahahahaha.
3. YES!!!!
4. Depends on where we're going.

4. Do you like being in charge but also causing a little **TROUBLE** behind the scenes?

1. It all sounds exhausting.
2. I like being in charge *because* I cause trouble!
3. I just like being in charge. The rest is irrelevant.
4. Yes—it's the only way to go!

5. Is it important to follow the **RULES**?

1. I do whatever's easiest.
2. It's important to follow *me*.
3. I will tell *you* the rules!
4. It's important to *appear* to follow the rules!

How dangerous is **MULTITASKING**?

6.
1. It should be outlawed.
2. It depends on the tasks.
3. JUST GET IT DONE!
4. As long as one of the tasks is throwing poo, it's fine.

Is good **NUTRITION** the key to feeling good?

7.
1. Napping comes first.
2. Being me is the key to feeling good.
3. I believe in being open-minded about defining nutrition sources.
4. Bein' FEISTY is the true key to feeling good.

Are you an **INSPIRATION** to the people who know you?

8.
1. "Inspiration" might be a strong word.
2. Duh.
3. YES!!!!
4. If I want to be an inspiration, I'll be an inspiration. Don't pressure me!

Do people come to you when they are looking for **ADVICE**?

9.
1. No. They do not.
2. Obviously. What do you want to know?
3. They don't have to come to me. I go to them.
4. Usually people come to me because I tell them to come to me.

What do you think of the saying, "Never do **TODAY** what you can put off until **TOMORROW**"?

10.
1. This is a FINE, FINE philosophy.
2. I would never do today what doesn't have to do with me.
3. JUST DO IT!
4. I would put off deciding if I was going to procrastinate until tomorrow.

SCORING:

For every time you chose answer 1, add 1 to your score.
For every time you chose answer 2, add 2 to your score.
For every time you chose answer 3, add 3 to your score.
For every time you chose answer 4, add 4 to your score.

RESULTS

WHICH FEISTY PET ARE YOU MOST LIKE?

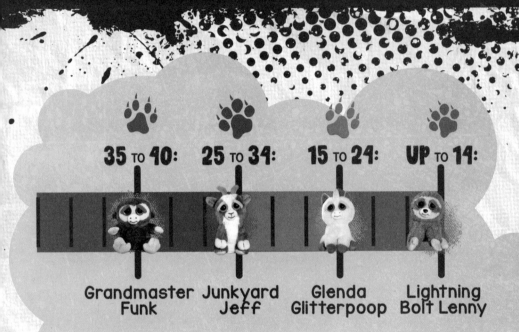

35 TO 40: Grandmaster Funk

25 TO 34: Junkyard Jeff

15 TO 24: Glenda Glitterpoop

UP TO 14: Lightning Bolt Lenny

GRANDMASTER FUNK!

35 TO 40:

You are an interesting mix of law-and-order and poo-throwing. Your next move is often tough to predict, but friends know you're always offering up something worthwhile.

JUNKYARD JEFF!

You are authoritative and outspoken. Nobody ever claims to not hear whatever it is you have to say. You encourage people no matter the situation. You always see the value of moving ahead!

25 TO 34:

GLENDA GLITTERPOOP!

15 TO 24:

You are always ready for the next party. Nobody knows better than you when it comes to hair, fashion, and generally looking fabulous. And everybody knows it!

LIGHTNING BOLT LENNY!

You are careful. Not likely to jump into anything too quickly. You will speak, but not until you've thought things through . . . or until you've woken up.

UP TO 14:

KOOKY CROSSWORD

Changing attitudes: What turns cute to feisty?

ACROSS

4. When triceratops get cranky, they use these to fight.
5. What kind of ache would be extra painful for a narwhal?
6. What kind of fruit would a Feisty Pet *never* bring for their teacher?
8. Raccoons are happy when they are eating this.
11. What sport is a feisty kangaroo good at?
12. What sound does a goat make when it's unhappy?
14. Horses express their moods using their ears, eyes, and _____.
15. An adult harp seal eats as much as 50 pounds of this a day!
16. What sport do short-legged, thick-bodied basset hounds hate?
17. This kind of rub makes a dog smile.
18. Three-toed sloths are really only happy in this kind of tree. (Hint: Unscramble these letters: CERPACOI)
20. What do butterflies use to determine the taste of something?
21. Knick-knack paddywack give a dog a _____ (if you want him happy).
23. This fruit makes two-toed sloths REALLY happy.
25. Turtles get feisty when you try to force them out of this.
27. Scratch behind this on a cat and you'll make it happy.

DOWN

1. Guinea pigs make this noise when they're happy.
2. Monkeys love them, and they're good for them (and you) too!
3. What do llamas do when they're feeling feisty?
4. When a polar bear wags this from side to side, it wants to play!
7. Which big cat is considered the second most aggressive (feisty!)?
9. When do horned owls most like to hunt?
10. Eating off the ground is annoying for giraffes because their legs are longer than their _____
13. What a pig happily snuffles through in search of tree roots.
17. What kind of forest gets pandas excited?
18. This substance makes cats very happy!
19. Penguins collect these to show their love (and build nests.)
22. What kind of leaves do koalas hate?
24. To stay healthy, snow leopards can do this for up to 18 hours a day!
26. What does a happy rabbit eat mostly?

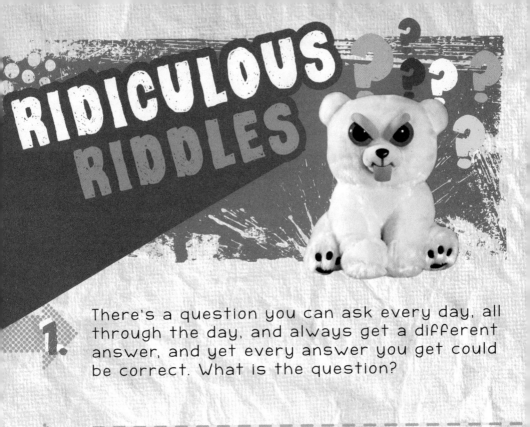

RIDICULOUS RIDDLES

1. There's a question you can ask every day, all through the day, and always get a different answer, and yet every answer you get could be correct. What is the question?

---

2. Spell a five-letter word that's a tasty treat just by using the letters C and Y.

---

3. Can you spell Feisty Pet backward?

FEROCIOUS FILL-INS

Here's another chance to write your own feisty story by filling in your own words! Create a list of words using the prompts below, then turn the page and use them to fill in the blanks.

GAME _____

ANIMAL _____

ADJECTIVE _____

ANIMAL _____

VERB _____

FOOD _____

NOUN _____

EMOTION _____

NOUN _____

NOUN _____

EMOTION _____

VERB _____

ADJECTIVE _____

ANIMAL _____

BODY PART _____

NOUN _____

BODY PART _____

ADJECTIVE _____

FOOD TYPE _____

NOUN _____

VERB WITH "-ING" ENDING

_____

SOME FEISTY ADVICE!

Crazy quotes from the Feisty Pets themselves!

"Playing _____ with a _____ is a _____ idea."
[GAME]   [ANIMAL]   [ADJECTIVE]
—Extinct Eddie

"Never ask a _____ to _____ the candles on a
[ANIMAL]   [VERB]
birthday _____."
[FOOD]
—Ferdinand Flamefart

"You can never have too much _____" —Glenda Glitterpoop
[NOUN]

"Money can't buy _____, but it can buy a _____."
[EMOTION]   [NOUN]
—Ice Cold Izzy

"Before approaching a _____, ask yourself, 'Do I feel _____
[NOUN]
_____?'"
[EMOTION]
—Karl the Snarl

"Never _____ the _____ road." —Katy Cobweb
[VERB]   [ADJECTIVE]

"Don't judge a _____ by its _____."
[ANIMAL]   [BODY PART]
—Lightning Bolt Lenny

"Never trust a _____ with your _____." —Liza Loca
[NOUN]   [BODY PART]

"Eat _____ preservatives and artificial _____
[ADJECTIVE]   [FOOD TYPE]
ONLY!"
—Princess Pottymouth

"Make sure no one is in the _____ before _____ it . . ."
[NOUN]   [VERB WITH "-ING" ENDING]
—Sir Growls-a-Lot

48

OBSERVATION
CHALLENGE

Put your powers of observation to the feisty test. Stare at this Feisty Pet scene. When you think you've really studied all the details in this picture, turn the page.

HERE'S THE SAME PICTURE . . . ALMOST!

There are five differences between the picture on the previous page and this one. Can you find them?

SILLY SPELLING

Find the name of a Feisty Pet by connecting letters in the box below. You can move sideways, diagonally, and up or down, and you can use letters more than once. There may also be letters that aren't used.

1.

S	A	I
C	R	N
S	E	I

_ _ _ _ _ _ _   _ _ _ _

2.

O	C	A
L	A	L
Z	I	Z

_ _ _ _   _ _ _ _

WILD WORD SEARCH

```
G R A C E F U L E T U C G C D
T U D C E L B A I C O S N H L
E L T N E G B U Y Z Z D I A I
H J H G N I G A G N E O L R M
E N J O Y A B L E L J Y A M G
D A R L I N G Y I E L L E I R
L O V E L Y K G Z D R G P N A
G N I T N A H C N E N G P G C
L D C B L T D E E I N L A H I
A A P U F O I O R L E A E M O
I I O U D R V A R A B E M F U
D N L D F D E I S A R A U U S
R T I K N D L A N F B Z I X H
O Y T S N I N Y U G Z L L M E
C Y E E X T K L J Y M H E H A
```

ADORABLE

AGREEABLE

AMIABLE

APPEALING

CHARMING

CHEERFUL

CORDIAL

CUDDLY

CUTE

DAINTY

DARLING

DELIGHTFUL

ENCHANTING

ENDEARING

ENGAGING

ENJOYABLE

FRIENDLY

FUZZY

GENTLE

GRACEFUL

GRACIOUS

HUMANE

KIND

LOVELY

LOVING

MILD

PLEASANT

POLITE

SOCIABLE

The opposite
of feisty
is . . .

WHO SAID IT?

Match the Feisty Pet with the quote that suits them. Then, fill in their speech bubbles.

Speed is my middle name.

If it's white and fluffy, I want it.

Don't make me your seal of approval!

I love you . . . to DEATH!

This is a job for Super Doofus!

Let the bunnies hit the floor!

Life is a box of chocolates—eat them all!

Don't be a boar!

Little white pony is OUT!

Livin' the feisty life!

I sleigh every day, bro!

Don't be a copycat!

Grandmaster Funk

Mary Monstertruck

Princess Pottymouth

Rude Alf

Suzie Swearjar

Vicky Vicious

Taylor Truelove

Tony Tubbalard

Louie Ladykiller

Glenda Glitterpoop

ir Growls-a-Lot

Karl the Snarl

55

ANSWERS

PAGE 4-5 A SECRET MESSAGE:

If you want to look smart to your friends, the easiest way to do that is to turn to the back of this book and look at the answers. But we do not endorse cheating or being lazy, unless you want to be a blockhead or a couch potato for the rest of your life!

PAGE 6-7 MATCH THE FEISTY PET:

Billy Blubberbutt (Spearfishing), Buford Buttsniffer (Eating poo), Dolly Llama (Spitting), Ebeneezer Claws (Stealing candy from babies), Ferdinand Flamefart (Playing with fire), Glenda Glitterpoop (Staring at mirrors), Grandmaster Funk (Throwing poo), Jacked-Up Jackie (Kickboxing), Junkyard Jeff (Screaming), Lightning Bolt Lenny (Hanging out)

PAGE 8-9 UNSCRAMBLE:

LETHAL LENA, VICKY VICIOUS, LUNATIC LEXI, TONY TUBBALARD, ICE COLD IZZY, SCARIN' ERIN, JUNKYARD JEFF, PRINCESS POTTYMOUTH, KATY COBWEB, SUZIE SWEARJAR, EXTINCT EDDIE, RUDE ALF

PAGE 12 WORD SEARCH:

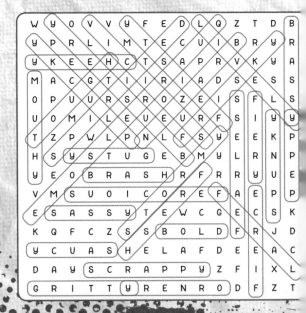

PAGE 14 STORY PROBLEMS:

1. Nellie lives in the Southern Hemisphere—seasons are opposite from the Northern Hemisphere.

2. The two mothers and two daughters are a grandmother, mother, and daughter.

3. Cool.

4. Sid is thirty.

5. Polly is 16 (The first letter of each name equals the number of where that letter falls in the alphabet.)

6. It costs 65 cents. (Each vowel is worth 5 cents and each consonant is worth 10 cents.)

PAGE 18 OBSERVATION SKILLS:

"70's" on Jukebox switched to "80's" / Narwhal's eyes changed color / Stars removed on plate / Jam on toast / Fork missing from in front of narwhal

PAGE 19 FIGURE PROBLEMS:

A. 12 (Add 4 to each number.)

B. 16 (Subtract 1 from the first number, 1 x 2 = 2 subtracted from the second number, 2 x 2 = 4 subtracted from the third number, 4 x 2 = 8 subtracted from the fourth number, and 8 x 2 = 16 subtracted from the fifth number.

C. 38 (Add 8 to each number.)

D. 534 (Each number descends by one for each step.)

E. 3 (Each row multiplies the two outside numbers and the answer is the two middle numbers.)

PAGE 20-21 CROSSWORD:

PAGE 26-27 OPTICAL ILLUSIONS:

It depends on how you count them all! From the top or the bottom, left or right, they are all impossible . . . just like being cute and feisty at the same time!

PAGE 28-29 MAGICAL CREATURE MYSTERY:

A gray elephant from Denmark

PAGE 30-31 REBUSES:

1. goofing around
2. batter up
3. run through the sprinkler
4. working around the clock
5. lying on the beach
6. lying under oath
7. being on time
8. swimming under water
9. side by side

PAGE 32-33 MAZES:

START

FINISH

START

FINISH

START

FINISH

PAGE 34–35 WACKY WORD GAMES:

Anagrams: eat/tea, dare/dear, pots/stop, teacher/cheater

1. Henry. He's the only one without an "I" in his name.

2. The first group of Feisty Pets each has a silent consonant in their name. So does Lightning Bolt Lenny.

PAGE 36 FEISTY WORDS:

funny, inexcusable, irritating, sassy, naughty, salty, disrespectful, indecent, terrific, silly

PAGE 37 CREATE WORDS:

40 possible solutions: EYE, FLIP, FLIT, FLUTE, FLUTTER, FLY, FRET, FRIES, IF, IRE, LEST, LIE, PIER, PITS, PREY, PRY, PURSE, REST, RIP, RIPE, RUSE, RUST, SEE, SIP, SIT, STEEL, STIR, STRIP, SUET, TEST, TIER, TIP, TREE, TRUST, UP, USE, YET, YES, YIP, YUP (and there may be others!)

PAGE 38–39

TRIANGLE PUZZLE:

Original:

Solution:

LICENSE PLATE MATCH-UP:

I GROWL. = Sir Growls-a-Lot, I AM QT. = Glenda Glitterpoop, TRTLPWR = Louie Ladykiller, SLOGO = Lightning Bolt Lenny, 18POOP = Buford Buttsniffer, TOP R8D = Ali Cornball, WHOOOOOO = Henry Whodunnit, I B IC = Ice Cold Izzy

Crossword grid (letters as filled in):

```
              W       B     S     H O R N S
    T O O T H         A P P L E
              I       N           E
              S       A     I     A
                      N     T     D
        A N Y T H I N G
    L       I         L     A         N
    I       I         L     A         N
B O X I N G           E     S C R E A M
    N       H               C       U
    N O S T R I L S         K       D
            T               F I S H
    S W I M M I N G     G
            M               B E L L Y
        C E C R O P I A
            A       E   M
F E E T     N       B   B O N E
            I       B   O
    D       I       L   O
G R A P E S         E
        L           S H E L L
    E A R   E
    D       E           A
            P           Y
```

PAGE 46 RIDDLES:

1. "What time is it?"

2. Candy

3. f-e-i-s-t-y-p-e-t-b-a-c-k-w-a-r-d

PAGE 50 OBSERVATION:

One side of colors changed on the Rubik's Cube / Cap of bottle changed color / Color altered on banjo neck / Flower vase on ledge behind couch missing / Pillow added behind the blue one

PAGE 51 LETTER GRID:

1. Scarin' Erin

2. Liza Loca

PAGE 52-53 WORD SEARCH:

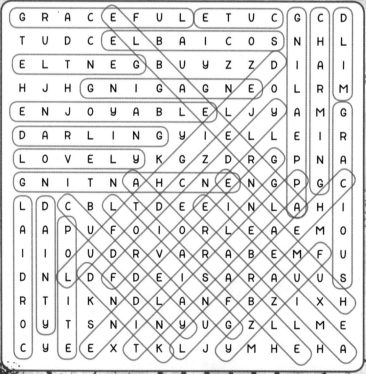

Grandmaster Funk: Livin' the feisty life!

Mary Monstertruck: Don't be a copycat!

Princess Pottymouth: Life is a box of chocolates—eat them all!

Rude Alf: I sleigh every day, bro!

Suzie Swearjar: Don't be a boar!

Vicky Vicious: Let the bunnies hit the floor!

Taylor Truelove: I love you . . . to DEATH!

Tony Tubbalard: Don't make me your seal of approval!

Louie Ladykiller: Speed is my middle name.

Glenda Glitterpoop: Little white pony is OUT!

Sir Growls-a-Lot: This is a job for Super Doofus!

Karl the Snarl: If it's white and fluffy, I want it.

IYETSF!